Count the Ways, Little Brown Bear

JONATHAN LONDON

illustrated by MARGIE MOORE

SCHOLASTIC INC.

New York Toronto London Auckland Sydney
Mexico City New Delhi Hong Kong Buenos Aires

ISBN 0-439-46009-3

12 11 10 9 8 7 6 5 4 3 2   2 3 4 5 6 7/0

Printed in the U.S.A.   09

First Scholastic printing, November 2002

Designed by Sara Reynolds

For sweet Maureen

J.L.

For Kenny

M.M.

Mama Brown Bear and Little Brown Bear
were eating a picnic supper in Bear Valley.
"Do you love me a lot?" asked Little Brown Bear.
"Yes," said Mama Brown Bear. "You can count the ways."

"I love you," she said,
"more than you love to eat
a sweet berry pie."

"Just **ONE**?" cried Little Brown Bear
as he gobbled down a whole juicy pie.
"Is that all?"

"No, that's not all.
I love you," said Mama Brown Bear,
"more than you love to catch
this striped fish
and this spotted fish."
"That's **TWO** fish," said Little Brown Bear.

"Right," said Mama Brown Bear.
"And I love you more than
I love to rub my back
against this tree...

and this tree...

and this tree. *Mmm, ahh*."

"That's **THREE** trees!"
said Little Brown Bear.

"And that's *still* not all," said Mama Brown Bear
as they strolled toward home.
"I love you more than you love
two green apples
plus two red apples.
Want one?"

"Not one—all **FOUR**!" cried Little Brown Bear.
And he ate them all—
crunch munch munch crunch.

"Well, I love you," said Mama Brown Bear,
"more than I love
   six honey jars,
   take away one honey jar."
"That's **FIVE** honey jars," said Little Brown Bear.
"But why did you take one away?"

"To give to you!" said Mama Brown Bear.
"Yum!" said Little Brown Bear.
"But I'm getting full," he said with a yawn.

"Looks like it's time for bed," said Mama Brown Bear.
"Not yet!" cried Little Brown Bear.
"I want to stay up and count
    the ways you love me."

Mama Brown Bear smiled.
"I guess we could do a little more."

"I love you more
than you love three counting books
and three bedtime books."
She read them all to him.
"That's **SIX** books," he said. "Can we read another?"

"Go to sleep now," said Mama Brown Bear,
tucking him in.
"Wait!" said Little Brown Bear. "Where are my teddy bears?"

"Here they are," said Mama Brown Bear.
"They're hiding under the covers."

"I love you as much
  as all of these teddy bears
  giving you bear hugs," said Mama Brown Bear.

"One…   two…   three…   four…

five…   six…   **SEVEN!**"

counted Little Brown Bear.
"Not enough!"

"Then add one more," said Mama Brown Bear.
And she gave him a great BIG bear hug.
"That's **EIGHT**," said Little Brown Bear.
"Still not enough!"

"Okay, silly," said Mama Brown Bear.
"I love you more than
   you love all my bedtime kisses."

"One...two...three...four...five..." *(yawn...)*

"six...seven...eight..." *(stretch...)*   "**NINE**..."

said Little Brown Bear, closing his eyes.

1 2 3 4 5

But then Little Brown Bear's eyes
shot back open, and he shouted,
"I love *you* more than
five plus five!"
He held up the claws on both front paws
and roared, "THAT'S **TEN!**"

6 7 8 9 10

Mama Brown Bear laughed.
Then, in a whisper, she said,
"I love you more
than all the stars in the sky."
Little Brown Bear smiled and
turned toward the window.
And before he
could count even ten stars…

he fell fast asleep.

z z z z z z z z z